THE SLEEPING
GIANT MOUNTAIN

Sharon Underwood

Chapter One

"WAKEY WAKEY, DOULTON!!!!" sang Charlie, whilst bouncing on Doulton's bed. "We're going on holiday!!!" "Ouch. Get off me, Charlie!" shouted Doulton, as he grumpily pulled his quilt over his head. Two seconds later, Doulton sat bolt upright and with a huge grin announced, "Charlie, we're going to Spain on a big adventure!" Doulton, wearing his favourite camouflage pyjamas, sprang out of bed and immediately took charge. "Charlie, you need to start packing." Charlie gathered all his favourite items and placed them in a heap on his bed. "Doulton, can you check what I am taking please?" There were marbles, balloons, a colouring book and pencils, a water bottle, a torch, a collection of white pebbles and his favourite dinosaur mask. "The pebbles will be too heavy. You'll find white pebbles in Spain. Anything else?" Charlie pointed above his bed to his dream catcher. "Do you really want to take that?" "Yes. I don't want to have bad dreams in Spain." Sometimes, Charlie would scream so loud that Doulton would wake with a jolt and either join in screaming or fall out of bed!

A large black snake with bright yellow eyes and huge poisonous fangs lived under the house. The snake would hide in the shadows until dark, then slowly slither up the drains and into the toilet. The dream catcher never failed and would catch the nightmare in exactly the same place…. but just in case, Charlie always flushed the toilet three times and double-checked the toilet seat was firmly closed.

Doulton stood on Charlie's bed but, no matter how much he stretched, he simply couldn't reach the dream catcher. "I'll help!" exclaimed Charlie and both boys began bouncing. It was impossible. The bed was so squishy, they either clashed and fell or completely bounced off the bed. Doulton was determined not to fail. He stopped bouncing, closed his eyes and began taking long deep breaths. Then, bending both knees, he made one huge final leap and punched the dream catcher off its hook.

They were ready and packed for their holiday. "Bye house, bye Chesterfield and bye church with the crooked spire," whispered Charlie. His mother put her arm around his shoulders. "Don't be sad, Charlie Chipmunk. You'll see Dad in a few hours and we'll begin our exciting summer adventure!" Charlie's nickname was Chipmunk, due to the fact he could store huge amounts of water in his rosy red cheeks. Charlie held the family record for spitting water in a long straight line for nearly 15 seconds.

They sat together near the front of the plane, excitedly waiting for take-off but, within five minutes, both boys had fallen fast asleep. Their mother gently woke them as the plane started to descend. Huddling together, they peered through a small round window.

"I can't see anything! Everything is white! The plane is covered in cotton wool!" whined Charlie, pressing his nose against the window. "That's not cotton wool, it's a cloud!!!"

Doulton spotted his father first, waving from the back of the crowd. "Dad!" they screamed, as they ran towards him. Poppy, the family dog, was so excited she started to spin. She spun round and round until she became so dizzy, she collapsed in a heap on the floor, facing the wrong way.

"I've missed you so much, Poppy Pooper," said Charlie, planting a sloppy kiss on her head and tickling her scruffy beard. "You'll love the villa, boys. It has a huge swimming pool." Charlie's lip started to tremble. "But Dad, you know I can't swim." "I know, Chipmunk, but don't worry. I have a surprise for you both."

Once Poppy and the suitcases were loaded into the car, they set off on the final part of their journey. "Dad, stop! Let's pick purple baseballs off the trees!" Puzzled, his father frowned at the rows and rows of trees and then exploded with laughter. "Charlie, those aren't baseballs. They're mangos!"

All at once, the boys were flung against their seats as the road began to climb rapidly. Finally, as they reached the very top, Doulton exclaimed, "Wow! Do monsters live in that lake, Dad?" "Monsters don't live in lakes." "They do!" stated Doulton, defiantly. "What about the Loch Ness Monster? I've seen hundreds of photos, so I know it's true!" The enormous lake glistened and shimmered like a mirror. "The water in the lake seems very low," commented their mother. "I think the lake desperately needs some rain." "Don't say that, Mum! We don't want any rain until we've gone back home!" cried Charlie. "Look at that mountain over there, boys. If you stare at the ridge, it looks like a huge man relaxing on his back. The locals call that mountain "The Sleeping Giant." "Please can we go and meet him, Dad?" pleaded Charlie, making everyone laugh. Their journey continued along windy country roads until, finally, they reached a pretty white village surrounded by a huge green forest. "Two minutes along this track, boys, and we're home!"

Chapter Two

The moment the car drew to a halt, the boys instantly jumped out and ran to the gate. Upon entering, they gazed up at an enormous monkey puzzle tree, towering high above the roof of the villa. Their eyes were then instantly drawn to a huge blow-up parrot, gently swaying and bobbing in the centre of the pool. The villa was U-shaped with a central courtyard overlooking the swimming pool. Inside the courtyard was a large metal pergola. "This is great. We could close all the curtains and hide in this, Charlie!" "Boys!" shouted their father. The boys dashed into the lounge and their father presented them both with brand new water pistols. Charlie squealed with delight, clapping his hands. "And Charlie, you won't need to worry about swimming in the pool. You can ride Peter the Parrot." "Let's test our water pistols, Charlie!" shouted Doulton. "Not so quick, boys! Spain is a very hot country and the sun burns your skin. You must always wear sun cream." "No," replied Doulton grumpily, "that's for girls." "Ah, my little soldier. I have some very special cream which the army use. It is green and brown and camouflages their faces." "Wow, mum. How did you get it?" asked Doulton, impressed. "I can't tell you as I am sworn to secrecy but let me know when you need some more," she whispered.

Charlie made a disgusted face as Doulton happily smeared dirt-coloured gunge all over his cheeks. "Don't worry, Charlie, you can use a clear one," laughed their mother. Doulton loved the army, ninjas, climbing and adventure. He also liked being in charge, especially of his little brother. Charlie didn't mind and loved playing with his bossy big brother, although sometimes, it was safer to hide when Doulton was in his crazy ninja mood. "Which bedroom is ours?" Doulton asked, wanting to unpack his rucksack. "You and Charlie can have the large bedroom by the monkey puzzle tree." "What did you bring?" Charlie asked. "I brought my army survival pack. I have rope, a water bottle, camouflage cap, walkie talkies, Poppy's water bowl and some magic sweets from the air hostess that stop your ears hurting."

Chapter Three

Charlie woke early the next morning, to the sound of tinkling bells and immediately sat up shouting, "WAKEY WAKEY!" until Doulton finally yawned and opened his eyes. "Listen to the bells, Doulton!" The boys raced through the villa and out to the far side of the swimming pool. Climbing the wooden fence, they managed to lean over and see the dirt track below. Huge bullocks with enormous horns were slowly ambling along the track, their bells tinkling with every step. Following behind was an old Spanish farmer and five scruffy dogs. The farmer leaned heavily on a long, crooked stick whilst the scruffy dogs ran from side to side, barking at the bullocks' heels. "Eeeeeeeeeeeeeeeeeeeeeahhhhhhhhh!" shouted the farmer. "Ayyyyyyyyyyupppppp!!!" shouted Charlie in reply. The old farmer looked up and smiled. His face was covered with a thousand criss-cross lines. "Hola." They watched the old farmer hobble along the dusty track and continue through the olive groves. Doulton asked his mother what "hola" meant. "Hello," she explained and Charlie began practising his new Spanish word. "Mum, I don't think Poppy understands Spanish!"

Doulton and Charlie decided to place bowls of water just outside the gates. A few hours later, the boys heard the distant tinkling of bells and knew the bullocks had begun their long walk home. The scruffy dogs looked tired as they neared the gates, then, noticing the neat row of bowls, quickened their step and began thirstily lapping the water. The large bullocks stood grazing on the far side of the track, then very slowly and one by one, the bullocks turned and started to walk towards them. Charlie grabbed Doulton's arm and whispered, "Are they coming to eat us?" "No, but I think we should walk backwards very, very slowly." "They are so big. I'm scared, Doulton."

"Ok. After 3…1.2.3. RUNNNNNNN!" Both boys ran as fast as they could towards the villa. "MUMMMMMMMM !!!" Charlie screamed and instantly their mother appeared at the door. "Get back, Mum! Run faster, Charlie!" They hurled themselves through the doorway and collapsed in the hallway. The bullocks were now happily grazing on either side of the driveway and slowly edging their way closer and closer towards their front door.

"Don't worry, boys! Those bullocks aren't dangerous. They are more scared of us! Let's slowly walk towards them and guide them back up the driveway." Charlie and Doulton were horrified and looked at each other in disbelief. Why would their mother suggest walking towards those huge bullocks with enormous horns? "Where's Dad?" cried Charlie, thinking his mother had gone completely mad. "He's gone to buy eggs but don't worry, Chipmunk."

Slowly and calmly, their mother started walking towards the bullocks shouting, "SHOOOOO! SHOOOOO!" Amazed at his mother's bravery, Doulton took a deep breath, grit his teeth and quick-marched to join and protect his mother. Charlie hovered in the background, staying close to the front door. What if the bullocks were fed up of eating grass and decided to try a 5-year-old boy? In super slow motion, the bullocks began to turn and walk back up the driveway. "Aaaaaayyyyupppppp!" shouted Charlie, now confident the bullocks were retreating and he raced to join Doulton and his mother.

Finally, the old farmer appeared, gasping for breath and waving his long, crooked stick. "Eeeeeeaaaaahhhhhhh!" The bullocks instantly quickened their step and turned back onto the dusty track. "Adios!" shouted the farmer, flashing a toothless smile. Doulton's mother gently kissed him on the cheek, whispering, "My hero," and Doulton's heart filled with pride.

Later that day, the family decided to walk and explore the village. Charlie gasped with delight when he noticed white pebbles dotted along the hedgerows and quickly began filling his rucksack. Doulton patrolled the narrow, cobbled streets, checking for danger or wild animals. "Charlie, did you know that village houses are made of gingerbread covered with thick white icing?" Charlie was amazed and ran to the nearest white house. "Yuuuuk, it's disgusting!" shrieked Charlie and angrily grabbed his water bottle. "EEEEEOOOOOOW...Stop, Chipmunk!" cried Doulton, quickly ducking to avoid the spray of water. "I'm sorry! I was only joking!"

Their walk home was filled with interesting facts and stories. "Look, boys. We are completely surrounded by mountains. Straight ahead is The Sleeping Giant Mountain and behind us is the forest and natural park. Which mountain shall we explore first?" asked their father. "The forest and natural park!" shouted Charlie.

"This is like driving to the top of the world," shouted Doulton, as they bounced over the bumpy track leading up to the natural park. Doulton was dressed in his favourite camouflage shorts, matching camouflage cap and tee-shirt, plus, under his mother's strict instructions, he had smeared stripes of green and brown sunscreen over his face.

Charlie stared at his brother. "You look like a weird treeboy!" Laughing and shouting, the boys ran through the forest and stumbled upon a beautiful waterfall. The boys simply couldn't resist and jumped, fully clothed, into the river. "Dad, I don't understand. Why is there so much water here yet hardly any in the lake?" "Good question, Doulton. I have no idea." They wandered alongside the river until suddenly, the river came to a dead end. Their father noticed that the river split into two smaller rivers, one to the left and one to the right. The original river was blocked with huge rocks and large broken trees, creating a wall higher than a double-decker bus. "I think there must have been a landslide which created this natural dam." "Shall we start digging, Dad?" asked Charlie, but his father shook his head. "Too big a job for us, I am afraid. It would take lots of men and machinery to clear this."

Chapter Four

Poppy jumped clumsily onto Charlie's bed, accidentally banging his knee. "Ooouuuchhhhh! What is it, Poppy?" Poppy's teeth were chattering loudly and she kept glancing over her shoulder. "Are you cold?" Charlie tickled Poppy's chin and noticed that she was also trembling. Suddenly, Charlie heard strange noises; banging, dragging and lots of whooshing. "Doulton, wake up. Please wake up," he whispered, not taking his eyes off the window. Charlie crept silently out of bed and tucked Poppy under the covers. Cautiously peeping out of the window, Charlie could see the monkey puzzle tree thrashing backwards and forwards, with branches snapping and flying through the air. The howling wind raced around the villa, dragging sunbeds, chairs and huge pot plants and then, as if by magic, a sunbed began spinning and spiralling high into the night sky. Without warning, the sunbed stopped spiralling and fell at a tremendous speed, landing heavily in the pool. SPLOOOOSHHHHHH! Charlie gasped and hid behind the curtain. Taking a deep breath, he decided to sneak one more peek. Charlie couldn't believe his eyes. The entire contents of the pool had spiralled upwards and created a huge spinning cone. Suddenly, the water cone stopped spinning, hanging silently in the air, then dramatically fell from the sky. As the water crashed into the pool, a gigantic wave jumped out and slammed hard against the window.

Everything went quiet. Too quiet. Then Charlie noticed the floor had begun to shudder and shake. "THUD…. THUD…. THUD…." The noise was deafening. Charlie lost his balance and crashed to the floor, bouncing and rolling with every shudder. Eventually, the thuds began to move away, far into the distance.

The garden looked like a demolition site. Charlie tiptoed back into his bed, snuggling alongside Poppy. "What do you think happened, Pops?" Poppy yawned, licked Charlie's nose and wriggled back under the covers.

"Charlie, wake up!" Doulton demanded, standing over Charlie with his hands on his hips. "Why are you so tired?" "The wind kept me awake. It kept throwing chairs and sunbeds into the pool." "Really !?" Doulton stared at Charlie, wondering if this was the start of yet another nightmare. Doulton ran into the garden and stopped suddenly, flabbergasted. What a mess. His mother and father were covered in mud, dragging broken pots, tables and chairs from the pool. Everything was drenched with water, even the barbecue house. Spiky branches from the monkey puzzle tree were scattered all over the garden. "Help us tidy up, Doulton. How on earth did these get here?" His father stood scratching his head, staring at two large rocks perched on top of the barbecue house. "That wind must have been so strong last night… it could've smashed all our windows!"

"Dad, look up at the sky!" shouted Doulton. "It looks very angry!" Menacing dark black clouds swirled above them. "That's strange. The weatherman said it would be sunny!" "Eeeeeeeeeeaaaaaaaaaaaaaah!" "It's the farmer!" shouted Charlie, leaning over the fence. "Aaaayyyyyyup!!" Charlie wondered what was causing the farmer to stumble. There were large dents in the dirt track which looked like huge footprints. "Muy Mal…Muy Muy Mal!" shouted the farmer, waving his stick angrily. As Charlie looked down over the valley, he noticed many broken trees and more large dents. "Dad, what is 'muy mal'?" "It means very bad, Charlie. Why?" "It's what the farmer shouted when he waved his stick." "He's probably angry about the storm." Once they'd finally finished clearing the garden, Charlie whispered, "Doulton, I need to talk to you. It's top secret." Doulton grinned and quickly looked left then right before answering. "Ok. Meet me in the pergola in five minutes."

Chapter Five

Charlie desperately tried to describe what had he had seen but Doulton seemed unimpressed and simply shrugged his shoulders. "It was only the wind." "But it wasn't just wind, Doulton. I was really frightened and so was Poppy!" Doulton stared at his brother's worried face. "I know, let's put your dream catcher above your bed."

"Hello. Is anyone home?" Steve, the pool man had arrived to clean the swimming pool with his grandson Josh. Josh was staying with his grandparents for two weeks and enjoyed helping his grandfather clean pools. Whilst the grown-ups discussed the terrible storm, the three boys chilled in the pergola, guzzling home-made lemonade, chocolate chip cookies and bowls of delicious ice-cream. "Where is your grandad's house?" asked Charlie. "Behind yours but further up the mountain. It's surrounded by the natural park." "Cool!" said Charlie. "We went there the other day and walked through a river." "That's really close to my grandad's! We can see your villa and all the way down the valley.!" "Did you see the wind last night?" asked Charlie, hopefully. "No, I didn't but when I woke up this morning, there were large dents all over the valley which looked like enormous footprints!" Charlie gasped and glared at Doulton.

"Maybe we should keep guard tonight and see if the wind returns?" suggested Doulton, noticing the fear in his little brother's eyes. Their father overheard their conversation. "I don't think you'll need to keep guard, boys. Look how calm the sky is. Last night must have been a freak storm, that's all."

The boys wandered inside and found their mother making sandwiches. "Fancy exploring some ancient thermal springs today, boys?" "What are they?" asked Charlie. "Many people believe that thermal springs have healing powers." "Wow! You mean a magic spring that cures people?" asked Doulton. Their mother laughed and said that maybe there was a touch of magic. "Can Josh come to the thermal springs?" asked Doulton. Josh looked at his grandfather, who simply laughed. "Oh, go on then. I will have to cope on my own!"

As they drove towards the Sleeping Giant Mountain, Josh pointed out that the lower part of the mountain resembled a boot. The rock boot normally dipped its toe into the lake but this year the water was too low. The boys studied the silhouette of the mountain ridge. They could see the giant's nose, chin, Adam's apple and his large round stomach. "Does he ever wake up, Mum?" asked Charlie. "No. It is just a mountain, Charlie. The rocks create shadows which make it look like a sleeping giant." "How strange," commented their father. "It's a lovely day yet look at those dark black clouds circling around the Giant's head." "Maybe he has a bad headache," said Charlie, making everyone laugh.

The boys had downloaded a map and Josh, being the eldest, took the lead. They trekked along an ancient pathway until eventually, they discovered a bubbling river leading to a circular rock pool. The boys shrieked with delight and jumped in. "Wow. It's really, really hot and there's loads of bubbles…and it stinks of farts!!!!" shouted Doulton, as he held his nose. Their father laughed and explained that the disgusting smell came from sulphur and that thousands of years ago, Romans would bathe in these springs. Many people would sit in this water, hoping to be cured of their illness. "Well, everyone must have been very smelly in the old days!" exclaimed Charlie. Doulton jumped out and grabbed empty water bottles from their rucksacks. "Let's fill the bottles with stinky magic water!"

It was pitch black when they eventually returned to the villa. "Can Josh sleep over, Mum?" asked Doulton, yawning. As soon as Josh's grandfather agreed, both Doulton and Josh screamed wildly and raced outside. They leapt high above the pool and clutching their knees, shouted "Water bombs!" as they crashed into the water below. "Dive in, Charlie, otherwise you'll stay stinky and smelling of farts!" Doulton grabbed his water pistol and started shooting. "Come here, farty boy!" Charlie couldn't stop giggling and, filling his own water pistol, screamed, "Attack !!!!" and the water battle began.

Finally, the boys collapsed onto their beds. "Goodnight, my stinky friends!" whispered Doulton and they all fell fast asleep smiling.

"What's happening!?" hissed Josh, gripping the side of his bed. "Why are the beds shaking!?" Poppy jumped onto the middle of the bed, cowering between Charlie and Doulton, her eyes wide with terror. Silently, the boys slipped out of their beds and Charlie carefully hid Poppy under the bed covers. Josh peeped out from behind the curtains. The room suddenly shuddered and water sloshed hard against the windows. The wind was whistling and howling around the villa. "I'm scared!" Charlie wailed. "Why is it so windy?" asked Doulton. "My grandad hopes these freaky storms will fill the rivers. If the rivers stay dry, it will be very, very bad." "That's what the farmer said.... muy muy mal," cried Charlie. All of a sudden, a large grey object dived into the swimming pool creating an enormous wave and sending Peter the Parrot hurtling through the air. Hearing a panicked bark, Doulton shouted, "That's Poppy!" Charlie spun around and threw back the bed covers but Poppy wasn't there. "We have to save her!" Doulton cried. "She's hiding in the pergola and it's about to take off in the wind! Hurry! Charlie, get your water pistol!" Josh grabbed a torch and they ran outside. "Everyone hold hands!" screamed Josh. The wind was angry, flinging them backwards and forwards. "Hold tight, Charlie. Don't let go!" screamed Doulton.

"Poppy.... POPPPPPYYYYYY! POPPPPPYYYYY!" "Duck!" screamed Josh, as a chair flew through the air. Huge rocks and branches crashed into the pool. "This is a pool tsunami!!" bellowed Josh, as another wave threw him against a wall. Doulton's face drained of colour as he pointed upwards into the night sky. Charlie and Josh followed Doulton's trembling finger and looked up and up and up and up. "OMG!!! Is it a monster? Is it made of rock? It's so big," exclaimed Josh. "I think his rock finger is in the pool. Get the pistols!!!!" ordered Doulton." "Josh, use the hose pipe. Fire!!!" All at once, the wind stopped and everything was still. Poppy seized her opportunity and darted out from the pergola to behind the boys. The three boys ceased firing and once more looked up at the rock monster. The monster made a very soft strange noise. "Aaaaahhhhhhhhhh!" "Reload the water pistols" shouted Doulton "Keep firing!" Again, the strange soft noise "Aaaaaahhhhhhhh" followed by a noise which sounded like a long sigh. "Do you think he likes it?" "I don't know. Try it again! Fire!" shouted Doulton. Slowly, the rock monster began to move away from the villa. Thud.... Thud.... Thud.... Thud....

Exhausted, the three boys and Poppy collapsed into a heap on the floor. "Will he come back, Josh?" Charlie asked, his teeth chattering from the cold. "I don't know, Charlie, but it did seem to be less angry when we covered it with water." They tiptoed soundlessly into their bedroom wearing huge grins and giving each other silent high fives. Within seconds, all had fallen fast asleep, including Poppy.

Chapter Six

The following morning, the boys held an emergency meeting and decided the rock monster must remain a secret. Doulton, Charlie and Josh then stood to attention and whilst saluting, made a solemn promise never to tell. Josh's grandfather arrived after breakfast. "OMG! You were in the wars last night. It must have poured with rain and looks like you've had more terrible winds." "Yes, yet we didn't hear a thing! Did we, boys?" Remembering their solemn promise, they automatically shook their heads. "Luckily, I found Peter the Parrot sat on top of the barbecue house. I wonder how he got there, Charlie?" "I dunno, Dad," answered Charlie, chewing his lip. "Grandad, please can Doulton and Charlie sleep over tonight?" Josh pleaded. "Only if you help me clean some pools today. They can come after 5 pm."

Once Josh and his grandfather had left, their father asked them where they'd like to visit. "I know. Let's visit the Sleeping Giant!" said Doulton. "Yippeee!" cried Charlie, who promptly ran to find his rucksack filled with white pebbles. Parking at the base of the Sleeping Giant Mountain, they noticed how far the water was from the giant's rock boot. They set off at speed, but the higher they climbed, the rockier and more rugged the landscape became. "Brrrrrrr. Glad we brought our jumpers. It's getting colder the higher we climb!" laughed their father. It took another forty minutes to reach the top of the mountain, mainly due to the fact that Charlie kept searching for just one more white pebble. "Which part of the Giant are we standing on?" asked Doulton. "His tummy," giggled Charlie. "Come on, let's climb to the top of his nose!"

After jumping and dancing on the Sleeping Giant's nose, they skipped over the giant's Adam's apple and returned to his large rounded belly. "I have a great idea!" cried Charlie. He raced back to the giant's Adam's apple and started placing white pebbles in a ring just below. Charlie then carefully created a diamond shape directly beneath the ring and filled it with more white pebbles. "What are you doing, Charlie?" asked their mother. "Making a tie for the Sleeping Giant !!"

Once home, they quickly prepared for their sleepover. Bikes, walkie talkies, torches, rope, sun cream and water pistols were loaded into the car.

After they'd waved goodbye to their mother, Doulton, Charlie and Josh ran straight to the bedroom and quietly closed the door. "So, what's the plan?" whispered Josh. "We can spy on the rock monster from up here and find out where it comes from and what it wants," suggested Doulton. "Great idea," nodded Josh.

As soon as Josh's grandparents shouted goodnight, the boys started their preparations. They quickly exchanged tee-shirts for dark sweatshirts and both Josh and Doulton rubbed camouflage sun cream over their faces. Luckily, Charlie had packed his dinosaur face mask so didn't have to smear the disgusting gunge over his face. "Ok, let's sneak into position." Doulton hid with his brother behind the tool shed and Josh crouched behind the garage. They'd decided to create code names when using the walkie talkies. Josh chose Rocky, Doulton decided on Ninja D and Charlie was Chipmunk. Hiding in the dark, everything appeared normal and still. "Come in, Rocky. Any monsters? Over." "Negative, Ninja D. Over." Suddenly, the ground shook. THUD. The boys all held their breath. Four seconds passed, then another THUD. Four seconds then another THUD. "It's coming," Rocky hissed. Charlie shivered and huddled closer behind Doulton. "I think I can see it," Doulton whispered. "What's it doing?" "I can't see very well. It looks like it is stopping at every swimming pool and splashing the water," said Josh. "OMG! He is at our villa!" gasped Charlie. Doulton and Charlie watched helplessly as the rock monster threw heavy rocks, trees and branches into their pool, creating gigantic waves. The monster began moving his enormous rocky arms round and round in giant circles, creating an enormous spinning cone of air. "OMG! Did you see that, Ninja D and Chipmunk? The monster has created a hurricane! Over." Sunbeds, tables and Peter the Parrot were sucked into the hurricane and spun round and round, high above the pool. Dramatically, the rock monster dropped both arms and the hurricane immediately vanished. All the items that had been sucked into the hurricane suddenly froze in mid-air. Time seemed to stand still. Then, everything suddenly dropped. Sunbeds, rocks, tables and chairs, crashed into the pool, creating a gigantic wave which washed over the rock monster.

"Ahhhhhhhhhhhhhhhhhhhhhhhhhhhhhhhhhhhhhhhhhhhhhhhh hhhhhhhhhhhhhhhh!" "Did you hear that? Do you think he liked the water?" asked Charlie, still trembling. The walkie talkie sprang to life and Josh whispered, "The monster seems quieter now. I think he enjoyed that. Now nothing seems to be happening. Over." They all sat quietly, watching and waiting. The monster no longer seemed angry and slowly began to move away. They could hear the slow thuds and the snapping of trees, as it moved further down the valley. "Let's meet back in the bedroom, Rocky. Over," whispered Doulton and they quietly tiptoed back to the bedroom.

As they huddled together, they tried to make sense of everything they had seen. "It's as though the monster liked it," said Josh "Did you hear that ahhhhhhhhhh sound? I think it definitely likes water." "Or maybe he is just thirsty?" whispered Charlie, sleepily. Josh and Doulton stared at Charlie. "I think you might be right, Charlie. The rock monster wants some water!" Josh started excitedly, jumping up and down. "I have an idea! There's lots of water in the natural park!" "Great idea, Josh, but how could we possibly get a rock monster to the natural park?" All three sat deep in thought with their faces in their hands. "I'm tired. Can we make a plan in the morning?" yawned Charlie and instantly fell into a deep sleep. Five minutes later, Charlie began kicking his legs and shouting, "Get back!" Doulton gently rubbed his brother's arm. "What happened, Charlie?" "I dreamt the rock monster was following us. We kept shooting him with our water pistols but he just kept following. It was really scary."

Doulton turned on the bedside light and, grinning from ear to ear, exclaimed, "You are so clever, Charlie. That's exactly what we need to do!!"

Chapter Seven

"Bedroom meeting in 10 minutes," Doulton whispered, whilst finishing breakfast. "I have another plan. Well actually, Charlie dreamt the plan," said Doulton. "The rock monster likes water so if we want him to follow us, we must tempt him with water." "How!?" cried Josh and Charlie. "We stay here another night and wait for the rock monster to arrive at our villa. Then, we flash our torches to get its attention and when the monster is close enough, we'll shoot water and hopefully, it will follow us." "But I can't run very fast. The monster will catch me." "Charlie, we can use our bikes. I'll tie rope from your handlebars to my saddle." Josh was considering the plan and then slowly started nodding. "This plan might just work." Huddling in their secret circle, Doulton took charge and went over the plan. "Is everyone happy and knows what they must do?" Josh nodded and Charlie simply said, "Don't leave me behind. I don't want the rock monster to eat me!" "Promise," Doulton said, high-fiving his little brother.

Later that evening, the boys started yawning and acting very sleepy. "You boys need an early night," laughed Josh's grandmother and the boys promptly went to bed. They each packed their rucksacks and whilst waiting for the rock monster, they all accidentally fell asleep. Suddenly, they were all hanging onto their beds as the villa shuddered and shook. THUD.... THUD.... "It's on its way!!" They tiptoed outside and watched as the monster stood over Doulton and Charlie's pool. Frantically, they started waving their torches. The monster did not appear to notice. "What now?" hissed Doulton. "Wait," said Josh, as he grabbed his grandfather's extra-long water hose and aimed it at the rock monster. Slowly, the rock monster started to move towards them. THUD......SHAKE......THUD....

SHAKE…. Charlie held his chin to stop his teeth chattering. "Get the bikes, quick!" screamed Doulton. They pedalled as fast as they possibly could until they reached the corner, then forming a line across the track, raised their water pistols. THUD…THUD…THUD…. "Take aim and fire!" shrieked Doulton, blasting the rock monster with water. "Ahhhhhhhhhhhhhhhhhhhhhhhhhhhhhhhhhhhhhhhhh," it groaned. "Pedal as fast as you can, Charlie." THUD…SHAKE. "He's coming!!!!!!!" screamed Charlie, looking over his shoulder. "Nearly there, Charlie." They dropped their bikes, ran to the river and refilled their pistols. "KEEP FIRING!" "Ahhhhhhhhhhhhhhhhhhhhhhhhh," groaned the rock monster. All of a sudden, the thuds began to quicken. "Out of the way. It's noticed the waterfall!" shouted Josh. SPLOSSSSSHHHHHHH! The rock monster was in the river. Water began flying through the air whilst huge waves started to wash down the mountain and smash against the dam. As the rock monster stamped and sploshed through the river, the waves grew bigger and stronger. Waves bashed against the dam, over and over until, eventually, the dam started to crumble. The noise was thunderous as dirt, broken branches and rocks began surfing down the mountain on an enormous wave.

"OMG. Did you see that, Doulton!? It's wearing a tie! It's the Sleeping Giant, not the rock monster!" stammered Charlie.

Tiptoeing back into their bedroom, Josh grinned. "Can't wait until tomorrow."

Chapter Eight

The boys woke just as the sun began to rise. "Ants in your pants, boys?" laughed Josh's grandad. "Why are you up so early?" "Could I stay at Charlie and Doulton's today?" It was all agreed and the boys were dropped off back to their villa with Josh. Charlie ran in to his mother and gave her a big hug. "Please can we go to see the Sleeping Giant?" "Does everyone want to go?" Josh and Doulton eagerly nodded.

"Gosh, I don't believe it! Look at the river flowing into the lake. It's full!! It must've been all those storms!" exclaimed their mother. The boys gawped in wonder. "Look at the Giant's boot. It's dangling in the water again!!" shouted Doulton. The boys ran up the Sleeping Giant's face and stood staring at the tie of white pebbles. "Told you it was him," whispered Charlie. "Lunch is ready," shouted their mother, handing the boys delicious home-made lemonade and cheese sandwiches. "I think the Giant might be thirsty," said Charlie. He jumped up and ran back to the giant's face and carefully poured some magic water. The ground beneath him gave a little shake and there was a very quiet "ahhhhhhhhhhhhh." Charlie smiled and whispered, "You are welcome."

Everyone was happy. The lake was full. Church bells rang and fireworks lit up the skies.

The following morning, the boys sat, dangling their legs in the pool and heard the tinkling of bells. "Eeeeeeeeeeeeeeeeeeeeeeeeaaaaaaaaaaaahhh!" Charlie and Doulton ran to look over the fence. "Muy Bueno! Muy Bueno!!" shouted the farmer, as he waved his long, crooked stick. "Gracias hijos!! Muchisimas gracias." Their father was stood behind them. "What does that mean?" Doulton asked. "He is saying 'Very good and thank you very much, boys'. What is he thanking you for?" Charlie and Doulton both shrugged and muttered, "Dunno," and turned to the farmer, shouting "AAAYYYYYYYYYYYUPPPPPPP!!!" Then Charlie whispered into his brother's ear. "The farmer knows our secret!"

Two weeks later, it was finally time to say goodbye to their lovely Spanish home. Doulton awoke just as the car approached Chesterfield. "I can see the crooked spire!"

Charlie opened his eyes and lazily smiled, knowing he was nearly home. "I know why the church spire is crooked! It's because the Sleeping Giant stood over Chesterfield Church and moved his big rocky arms in huge circles and created a hurricane. The church spun round and round and round until the hurricane finally stopped but the spire was all twisted and crooked!" Doulton glared at his brother, shaking his head.

"It was a secret!"

Their mother burst out laughing. "Have you just woken up, Charlie?"

Lightning Source UK Ltd.
Milton Keynes UK
UKHW051051291220
375879UK00001B/4